TOO CUTE! BABY ANIMALS

BABY FARM ANIMALS

RACHAEL MORLOCK

PowerKiDS press

Published in 2025 by The Rosen Publishing Group, Inc.
2544 Clinton Street, Buffalo, NY 14224

First Edition

Editor: Rachael Morlock
Book Design: Michael Flynn

Photo Credits: Cover, p. 1 Andrew Linscott/Shutterstock.com; (series background) Viktoriia LiSa/Shutterstock.com; p. 5 Qvist2000/Shutterstock.com; p. 7 HunsaBKK/Shutterstock.com; p. 9 ADA_photo/Shutterstock.com; p. 11 Thuwanan Krueabudda/Shutterstock.com; p. 13 Jeffrey Schwartz/Shutterstock.com; p. 15 Rita_Kochmarjova/Shutterstock.com; p. 17 JoshuaDaniel/Shutterstock.com; p. 19 Rita_Kochmarjova/Shutterstock.com; p. 21 Marlinda vd Spek/Shutterstock.com.

Library of Congress Cataloging-in-Publication Data

Names: Morlock, Rachael, author.
Title: Baby farm animals / Rachael Morlock.
Description: [Buffalo, New York] : PowerKids Press, [2025] | Series: Too cute! Baby animals | Includes bibliographical references and index.
Identifiers: LCCN 2024004113 (print) | LCCN 2024004114 (ebook) | ISBN 9781499445206 (library binding) | ISBN 9781499445190 (paperback) | ISBN 9781499445213 (ebook)
Subjects: LCSH: Livestock–Juvenile literature. | Livestock–Infancy–Juvenile literature.
Classification: LCC SF75.5 .M678 2025 (print) | LCC SF75.5 (ebook) | DDC 636–dc23/eng/20240228
LC record available at https://lccn.loc.gov/2024004113
LC ebook record available at https://lccn.loc.gov/2024004114

Manufactured in the United States of America

CPSIA Compliance Information: Batch #CSPK25. For Further Information contact Rosen Publishing at 1-800-237-9932.

CONTENTS

On the Farm

Many farmers care for animals, and each animal has a job to do. They might help with **chores**, produce goods like wool, or supply food like eggs, milk, or meat. Farm animals usually have babies in the spring. Their first job is to be cute!

Chicks

What's cuter than a fluffy baby chicken? Chicks **hatch** from eggs at least 21 days after the eggs are laid. The chicks break open the eggshell with their feet and beak. Chicks are born with soft **down**. They grow new feathers in a few weeks.

Ducklings

Like chickens, baby ducks hatch from eggs. They use a special egg tooth on their beak to break their eggshell. Fuzzy down makes ducklings look extra sweet. New feathers grow in when they're about six weeks old. A **brood** of ducklings sticks together, on land and in water.

Piglets

A mother pig gives birth to a **litter** of about 10 babies! These piglets weigh just a few pounds each. Right away, they **scramble** to drink their mother's milk. Piglets grow quickly. By the time they're three weeks old, they weigh 15 to 20 pounds (7 to 9 kg).

Calves

A mother cow usually gives birth to one baby at a time. Her calf already weighs 50 to 100 pounds (23 to 45 kg) when it's born! The calf drinks its mother's milk at first. When it's older, the calf can eat grass and hay.

Foals

Baby horses are called foals. Usually only one foal is born at a time. A foal can stand up within an hour of being born. It's not long before it can walk and run too! The foal stays close to its mother and drinks her milk.

Lambs

Mother sheep often have twins. The lambs can stand and walk within an hour of being born. They are covered in very soft wool. Lambs form a strong bond with their mother. They drink her milk several times an hour, in between playing and sleeping!

Kids

Goats are often born as twins or even triplets. Goat babies are called kids. Much like human children, they are active and curious! Kids stand and walk shortly after birth. Soon, they're ready to run, jump, and play. The noises a goat makes are called bleats.

Spring Babies

Spring is a good time to meet baby animals on a farm. You might get to pet a lamb's soft wool, hold a **cheeping** chick in your hand, or hear a kid goat bleat. You can make plenty of cute, new friends on a farm!

GLOSSARY

brood: A group of newly hatched chicks.

cheep: To make a quick high sound.

chore: A task.

down: A covering of soft fluffy feathers.

hatch: To break open or come out of.

litter: A group of babies born to an animal at the same time.

scramble: To move quickly to get something before someone else does.

FOR MORE INFORMATION

BOOKS

Emminizer, Theresa. *Lambs*. Buffalo, NY: PowerKids Press, 2024.

Hinman, Bonnie. *Farm Animals*. Minneapolis, MN: ABDO Publishing, 2023.

Horning, Nicole. *Foals*. New York, NY: Cavendish Square, 2021.

WEBSITES

Barnyard Babies with Dr. Pol
kids.nationalgeographic.com/videos/topic/barnyard-babies-with-dr-pol
Watch these short videos from National Geographic to see baby farm animals at their cutest!

Kids' Farm Cow
nationalzoo.si.edu/animals/cow
Read more about cows and how they're used on farms.

INDEX